GROW YOUR MIND

BUILD RESILIENCE

Written by Alice Harman
Illustrated by David Broadbent

W
FRANKLIN WATTS
LONDON · SYDNEY

Franklin Watts
First published in Great Britain in 2020 by The Watts Publishing Group
Copyright © The Watts Publishing Group, 2020

 Produced for Franklin Watts by
White-Thomson Publishing Ltd
www.wtpub.co.uk

ISBN (HB): 978 1 4451 6930 9
ISBN (PB): 978 1 4451 6929 3
10 9 8 7 6 5 4 3 2 1

Series Designer: David Broadbent
All illustrations by: David Broadbent

Printed in China

Franklin Watts
An imprint of
Hachette Children's Group
Part of The Watts Publishing Group
Carmelite House
50 Victoria Embankment
London EC4Y 0DZ

An Hachette UK Company
www.hachette.co.uk
www.franklinwatts.co.uk

Facts, figures and dates were correct when going to press.

A trusted adult is a person (over 18 years old) in a child's life who makes them feel safe, comfortable and supported. It might be a parent, teacher, family friend, care worker or another adult.

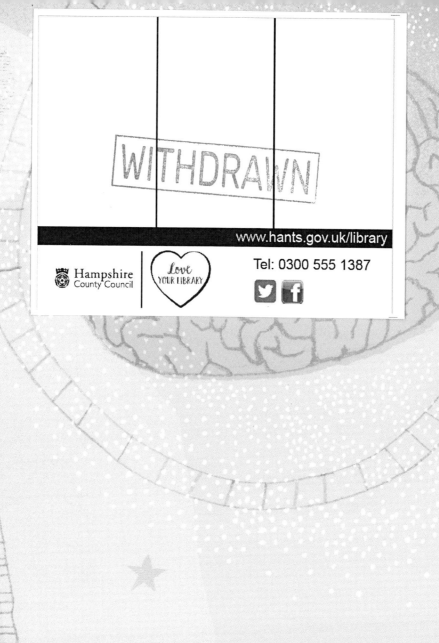

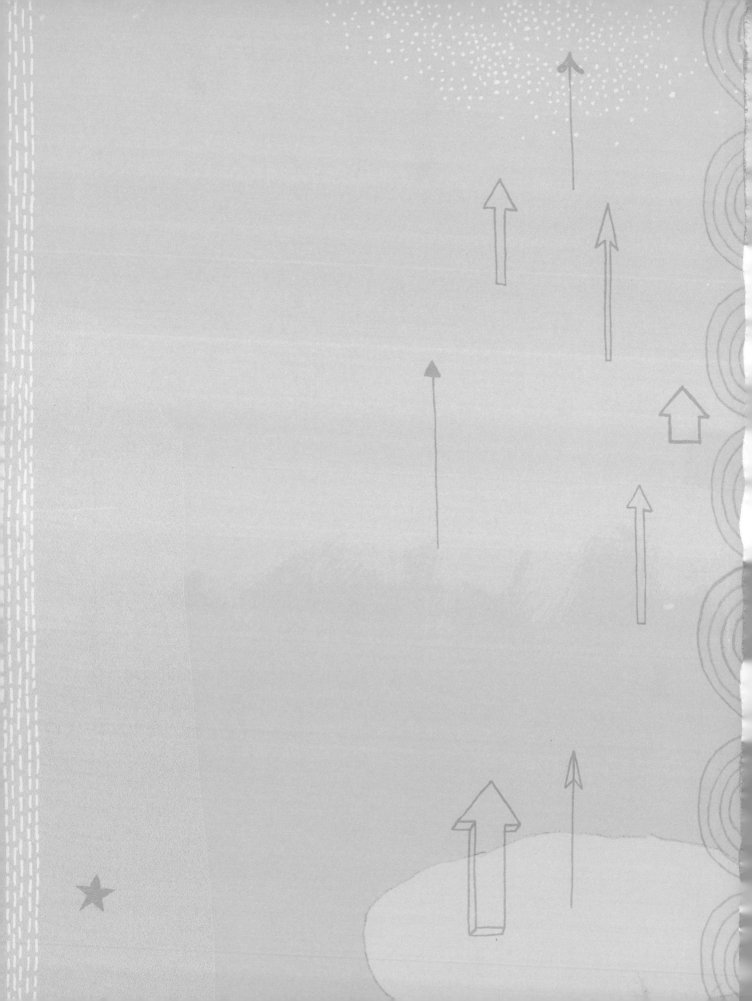

CONTENTS

A resilient mindset

Sometimes in life, things don't go exactly the way we want them to. We can find ourselves having to deal with all sorts of **frustrating, difficult or sad situations** – from struggling to understand a new subject in class to worrying about someone in our family being ill.

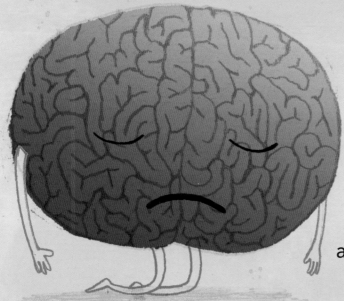

When things get tough, it can feel like we're stuck in that situation forever – like we'll never feel better and there's nothing we can do about it.

But, thankfully, this isn't how things have to be. You can't stop negative things happening to you, but you can learn to **build resilience**.

This means learning how to **keep going and stay positive** when things are really challenging. It also means helping yourself to recover more quickly from difficulties.

We often think of our brains as being fixed the way they are, but in reality they are always **growing and changing**.

Every person's brain has **billions of neurons**, which pass messages to each other along paths. Our thoughts and actions can help build new paths and strengthen ones that already exist.

This means that your brain can rise to new challenges – even ones that feel really hard and you'd rather not have to deal with – and **learn and grow** from them.

When we're resilient, we keep going even when things get difficult – this is called **persevering**. Although we may struggle during tough times, we know that with effort we'll bounce back and find future success and happiness.

The power of 'yet'

Have you ever tried to do something, not managed it, and thought, **'Argh, I just can't do it!'** How does it make you feel? Not great, right?

'I can't do it' can make us feel stuck – like things can't change, so there's no point in even trying. But that's not true – your brain is always changing and growing, and you can learn all sorts of new things. So instead of thinking 'I can't do it', try switching to **'I can't do it YET'**.

Adding 'yet' to a negative statement **unlocks a door** to a positive future, and encourages us to push it open. It builds our resilience by helping us to understand that difficult situations can change and get better.

Write down something that makes you think 'I can't do that'. It could be anything, from **reading a difficult book** to talking to a group of friends again after a big falling-out.

Put it into a negative sentence – for example, 'I can't read this book'. How does it make you feel? Pretty bad, right?

Now add the 'yet' – **'I can't read this book YET'**. How about now?

Believing that something could be possible in future encourages us to think, 'So how can I make it happen?' Come up with three 'I can' sentences to answer this question – for example, 'I can practise reading with my parents in the evening'.

Effort thermometer

It can be hard to **stay resilient** if we focus on the outcomes and achievements in our lives, rather than the efforts we've made. We might be disappointed and feel bad about ourselves, even if the negative outcomes are partly or entirely because of things that we can't control.

It can help to change our measure of success to focus on our behaviour – which we *can* control, even if things are difficult and not working out the way we hoped. This way, we can still feel **proud of and happy with ourselves**.

This approach makes us more resilient by encouraging us to keep going through difficult times, because what matters is how we act rather than what the outcome is.

Create an **'effort thermometer'** to track how much effort you've put into different challenges – from working through your fears and worries to getting on better with your brother or sister.

You can use the example thermometer on this page to get started – choose the section of the thermometer with the words and phrases that best describe how much effort you're making.

Remember, your **effort score** is personal to you – it depends on your mood, how you feel about the task and so on.

Keep an **effort journal** of your tasks, scores and what you learned. You should find that putting in more effort really does help you feel better and learn positive lessons, even if you can't yet see any difference in terms of outcomes.

4

Challenging myself

I find this very difficult but I'm trying my hardest

Concentrating

3

Trying to meet challenges set by others (teachers/family)

2

Mostly behaving well

Improving

1

I give up

Misbehaving instead of working

9

Digging deeper

Have you ever felt so frustrated with how long it's taking to do or learn something that you want to just **give up altogether**?

From making new friends to learning a new skill, it can be really difficult when things take a while – especially when they are important to us.

So how can we build our resilience to cope with these feelings of frustration? We need to stop worrying about doing things quickly, and instead see all the positives in giving ourselves time to **dig deeper** and make lasting change.

When we give things our **full, unrushed attention**, we may end up understanding them – and ourselves – much better.

Olivia

I used to have a **best friend** at my school,
and we had so much fun together that I didn't really
care about not spending time with anyone else.

But then he had to **move away.** Although we could still video call each
other in the evenings, everything changed. I was suddenly
on my own at school and I felt really lonely.

I knew a few people to chat to a bit, but it felt so awkward getting to
know them properly – like it would never be the same. I just wanted
to fast-forward to us being close friends already.

I talked to my mum and she told me that making good friends was like
building a house. You can build quickly on the surface, but the house
is much stronger if you dig deep foundations for it.

She helped me be patient enough to keep trying, rather than giving
up and staying lonely. I've got much closer to two friends now and
it feels real rather than forced.

Halfway there

A great way to **build your resilience** is to think about how everything you do helps develop your brain over time (see pages 4–5). You don't have to worry about making mistakes, or not doing things 'perfectly', because your efforts are still helping you along your lifelong journey.

Think about it this way – when you start looking at a **challenging new subject** in maths, are you starting completely from the beginning?

No! Because earlier in your life you've made efforts to learn what numbers are, how to add them together and other things that are helpful now. We call this your 'prior learning'.

Try out this activity to discover how your prior learning helps you reach your goals.

1. Draw a line of **five squares**, with a star in the middle square. Think about the challenge you're facing and write your goal in the final square of the grid.

2. In the squares before the starred middle one, write in the knowledge and skills that you've already worked hard to gain.

3. In the squares after the starred middle one, write in the steps you can take to reach your goal. You could ask an adult to help with this.

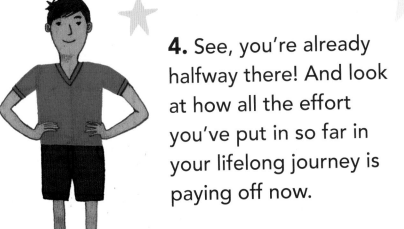

4. See, you're already halfway there! And look at how all the effort you've put in so far in your lifelong journey is paying off now.

Learned to write | Wrote my own poem | ★ | Write my own short story | Write a book!

Try to fail

Everyone makes mistakes, but we can often see them as failures. This might make us feel bad when we don't do something perfectly, and we may not want to try again.

In reality, learning from mistakes is a great way to give your brain a **big growing boost!** You can build your resilience by changing the way you think about mistakes, seeing them as opportunities to grow and learn.

Imagine dropping two balls on the ground – **one is inflated**, the other deflated. The deflated one can't bounce back up, but the inflated one can. If we see mistakes as failures, we feel down and deflated when we make them. But if we see mistakes as learning opportunities, it helps us to bounce back up – ready to try again!

Victoria

I was at a big family party a while ago,
and I was **showing off** a bit in front of my older cousins
because I wanted them to think I was grown-up like them.

I tried to use some of the longer words we'd learned in class recently,
but they were confused and laughed because what I'd said
didn't make sense – I'd got the meanings mixed up.

I felt so silly and embarrassed that I ran off to find my grandma.
I didn't want to go back out and see everyone.

When I told my grandma what had happened, she said she was really
happy that I was trying to **challenge myself** – and that with a bit of
practice I'd have so many more interesting words to use to express myself.

I went back out to the party and joked around with my cousins,
and they hadn't cared at all about my mistake – in fact, they were
worried they'd upset me. I learned **how brave** I can be – and
that people don't expect me to be perfect anyway!

POSITIVE PRACTICE

Sometimes, as hard as we try not to, we can feel **disappointed or frustrated** when things don't go our way.

One thing that can really help build our resilience for these moments is **'collecting' positive thoughts**. When things get tough, and it feels like everything is rubbish and only getting worse, we then have some positive examples to show us this isn't true.

By making an everyday habit of thinking about things to be grateful for or feel good about, you can **help your brain** bring them to mind much more quickly and easily in difficult times. This can give you a resilience boost to keep on thinking positively.

Try this

Every day, at a time when you're
together with some or all of your family,
each person takes a turn to share the
following positive experiences from their day:

1. One thing I did today that made someone else happy.

2. One thing that someone else did that made me happy.

3. One thing that I learned.

Later, try writing down the examples that stick in your
brain and that make you really believe things
can change for the better. When you next feel
down, have a look at this list for some
positivity inspiration.

Stronger together

Although developing your resilience can be really helpful and positive, remember that no one expects you to always be **tough and happy** – or to deal with everything all by yourself.

It's okay if things aren't okay, and your trusted adults want to know if you are struggling so they can listen and help. If anyone or anything is making you feel upset or worried, don't try to deal with it alone – always talk to a trusted adult.

It can often help you feel better just to **share the problem**, and other people may have great ideas that will help – ones that you'd never even thought of!

Hussein

When we moved to another city for my mum's new job last year, I found it really hard. We moved in the middle of the school year so I had to catch up on the work we were doing in my new class. **I felt lost**, and started worrying so much that I didn't really listen when the teacher was talking.

I didn't want to bother my mum – she was so busy with her new job and decorating the house. She told me how proud she was of me for doing so well, and I didn't want to disappoint or worry her.

But one day I had a bad stomach ache from worrying and I told my mum I didn't want to go to school.

We **talked over everything** and she wasn't disappointed at all – she just wanted to help me, so she was glad I'd told her about my problems. She talked to my teacher, and now we talk about my work and worries every day after dinner.

CHANGE FOR GOOD

When we're struggling with tough
situations, an important part of being resilient
is understanding that things can – and do –
change for the better.

Even if you're in a situation that you can't control,
like having to leave your friends behind when you move
house, there are all sorts of ways things can get better.
You can meet new people and discover new things that
you enjoy. You can also develop new ways of staying close
to your old friends, like sending each other videos.

We often feel nervous about change and would prefer
things to just stay the same. It can be really helpful
to get used to **thinking about change** as
something positive.

Try out these activities to practise seeing change as a normal and positive part of life. You might think up some of your own activities, too – that's even better!

1. Try one new thing a week – whether it's a food, an activity or listening to a song you've never heard before. Keep a journal of all the new things you've tried, and record what each experience was like. You might find some new favourites!

2. Let go of things you don't need any more – this could be old clothes that don't fit, or books and toys that you've grown out of. Ask a trusted adult to help you recycle them, donate them to a charity shop or pass them on to someone who can use them.

3. Think of something that you didn't really like when you first tried it – anything from an activity to a type of fruit. Give it another try! Because we're always changing, you might find that it's much better this time.

SEEING THE FUTURE

Don't worry, you won't need a crystal ball for this – just **your imagination**!

A great way of **building resilience** to deal with problems in the present is to learn how to visualise – that is, to create a picture in your mind – of a positive future.

Visualising a future version of yourself, at a time when you have overcome your problems, helps your brain to realise that it is possible to do so – that you're not stuck in a difficult present for ever.

When you feel really stuck or down, it can be hard for your brain to imagine things can get better. But if you practise this **visualisation** skill regularly, it should be easier to do when you need it most.

Toby

When my **uncle died suddenly**, it felt like it tore a big hole in my life. He was so funny and kind, and I missed him so much that it actually gave me a pain in my chest and stomach. I felt like I hadn't had a chance to say goodbye and like I'd never feel better about it.

My mum was **so sad**, too, and she asked me to try something called 'visualisation' that was helping her a lot. I imagined a picture in my mind of myself in future, smiling with my mum as we talked over all the good times we'd enjoyed with my uncle.

Visualising that future makes it seem more possible for me. Instead of feeling so stuck and scared, now I feel like I've got something positive to work towards.

I talk through my feelings regularly with my mum and other trusted adults, and I know it's okay to be sad and take time to move forwards.

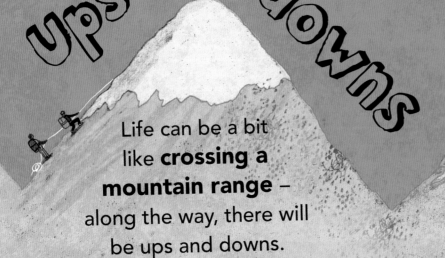

ups and downs

Life can be a bit like **crossing a mountain range** – along the way, there will be ups and downs.

When we're feeling good and things are going okay, it might feel like we're **at the peak** of a mountain. But when events in our life knock us off course, we may feel like we've slid right back down the other side.

If something really serious happens – like our parents splitting up or somebody we love dying, it might feel like we've slid down so far that we can't ever climb back up again. This is why it's so important to **build up resilience** – to help us keep trying anyway.

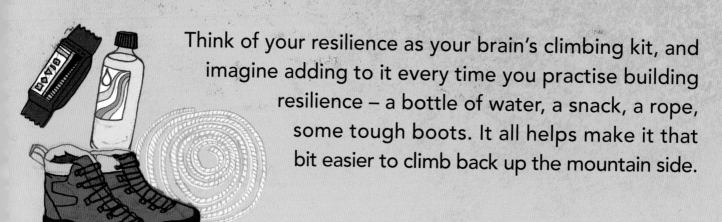

Think of your resilience as your brain's climbing kit, and imagine adding to it every time you practise building resilience – a bottle of water, a snack, a rope, some tough boots. It all helps make it that bit easier to climb back up the mountain side.

Kieran

When my dad told me and my brother he was **moving out,** and that he and my mum were getting divorced, I didn't want to believe it was true.

I didn't want to talk to anyone or do anything, and I got really angry and shouted if people tried to make me. It felt like everything would be worse from now on and there was **nothing I could do** about it.

Eventually my grown-up big sister helped me see that although things were hard now, we would all be **happy again** in future – even if that future was different to how I'd imagined it.

We made a plan of some activities to help me persevere when things felt really tough – from talking to trusted adults to listing all the things that I was still **thankful for.** This helped me to visualise a positive, realistic future.

Some days are still hard, but I'm coping and **feeling much better** now.

REST AND RECOVER

It's important to remember that **you're not a machine!** It takes effort to use your resilience to face challenges – whether that's new, big ones or just lots of little ones throughout the day.

We all need time to **rest and recover** from this hard work – we can't keep on going forever without ever having a break. Working non-stop can make us feel worn out and frustrated, and means our brains don't function well.

This may weaken our resilience to **cope** when things aren't going exactly as we'd hoped, making us more likely to think 'I can't do it!' and give up altogether.

And while you **take a break**, your brain might keep working on challenges for you anyway. Scientists have found that when we relax and stop consciously thinking about a problem, our brains carry on busily making connections between neurons on an unconscious level. **Thanks, brain!**

So what are your favourite ways to give your brain a lovely break?

Try to think of **five things** that make you feel really calm, or that are easy and fun to do. It could be colouring in, dancing around to your favourite song, playing outside, making up a story, watching cartoons – anything you like!

Make a small **'Brain Break'** reminder card. Write or draw your five ideas on this card and keep it in your pocket or bag. When you're feeling a bit worn out or frustrated, take out the card and try out one or more of the ideas.

Get creative

Sometimes if we're facing challenges in life and feel like nothing we try is working, it can be tempting to give up. A great way to build resilience is to learn how to **think a little differently**.

Looking at the world in creative ways can help unlock and wake up your brain, **building pathways** and sending neurons jumping into action.

You can practise your creative-thinking skills through all sorts of **fun activities** – including drawing, making up stories, inventing games and trying to solve riddles.

By helping your brain open up to more possibilities, you should find it easier to **think creatively** when you face problems that you're not sure how to solve.

Try out these activities to **spark your brain's creative power** – or, even better, make up your own!

1. Pick **three objects** you can see around you and make up a story that includes all of them.

2. Draw **three circles**, then turn them into anything you want – a face, an animal or maybe a spaceship!

3. Put on your inventor hat and think of three ways to make your **favourite game or toy** even more fun.

4. Think up some silly 'Would You Rather?' questions. For example, would you rather have **spaghetti for hair** or forks for fingers?

Keep BUILDING RESILIENCE!

Read through these tips for a quick reminder of how best to **build resilience!**

Instead of thinking 'I can't do that', try switching to 'I can't do that **YET'**.

Focus on the **efforts** you're making, rather than on their outcomes.

Aim to **slow down** and learn deeply rather than racing ahead.

Use your previous **life experience** to face new challenges.

See mistakes as **opportunities** to learn and grow.

Make it an everyday habit to **share positive experiences** with your family.

Talk to a **trusted adult** if you feel upset or worried – don't try to deal with it all by yourself.

Try **new experiences** and challenge your old, set ideas.

Visualise a **positive future** to help your brain imagine it being possible.

Keep on building your resilience even when things are **going well**, to help you learn how to deal with tougher times.

Discover what **calms you down** when you feel worn out and frustrated.

Practise your **creative thinking** and problem-solving in different, fun ways.

Notes for parents and teachers

The concept of a **'growth mindset'** was developed by psychologist Carol Dweck, and is used to describe a way in which effective learners view themselves as being on a constant journey to develop their intelligence. This is supported by studies showing how our brains continue to develop through our lives, rather than intelligence and ability being static.

Responding with a growth mindset means being eager to learn more and seeing that making mistakes and getting feedback about how to improve are important parts of that journey.

A growth mindset is at one end of a continuum, and learners move between this and a 'fixed mindset' – which is based on the belief that you're either clever or you're not.

A fixed mindset is unhelpful because it can make learners feel they need to 'prove' rather than develop their intelligence. They may avoid challenges, not wanting to risk failing at anything, and this reluctance to make mistakes – and learn from them – can negatively affect the learning process.

Help children develop a growth mindset by:

- Giving specific positive feedback on their learning efforts, such as 'Well done, you've been practising …' rather than non-specific praise such as 'Good effort' or comments such as 'Clever girl/boy!' that can encourage fixed-mindset thinking.

- Sharing times when you have had to persevere with learning something new and what helped you succeed.

- Encouraging them to keep a learning journal, where they can explore what they learn from new challenges and experiences.

- Making sure they understand that being resilient doesn't mean they're not allowed to feel worried or sad, it's just a way of helping them to recover and keep going.

Glossary

fixed mindset   thinking about your brain and intelligence as something fixed, and yourself and others as either clever or not clever

growth mindset   thinking about your brain as something that changes and grows, rather than something fixed that makes you either clever or not clever

neurons   cells in your brain that pass information back and forth between one another

persevere   keep going even when things get difficult

resilience   the ability to stay positive and make an effort even when things are challenging, and to recover quickly from difficulties

Index

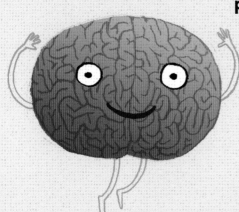

GROW YOUR MIND

978 1 4451 6860 9
978 1 4451 6861 6

978 1 4451 6923 1
978 1 4451 6924 8

978 1 4451 6925 5
978 1 4451 6926 2

978 1 4451 6927 9
978 1 4451 6928 6

978 1 4451 6930 9
978 1 4451 6929 3

978 1 4451 6931 6
978 1 4451 6932 3

978 1 4451 6933 0
978 1 4451 6934 7

978 1 4451 6935 4
978 1 4451 6936 1

Series contents

Boost Your Brain
- A brain-boosting mindset
- Sshhhhhhh...
- One thing at a time
- Think, rest, repeat
- Brain hugs
- Time out
- Take care of your body
- Brain dump
- Picture this
- Sum it up
- Make a mnemonic
- Study buddies
- Brainy book

Make Mistakes
- Mistakes and mindsets
- Feeling down
- Think again
- Types of mistake
- A new strategy
- A-ha!
- A healthy brain
- Time to shine
- Trying new things
- Don't give up
- Challenge o'clock
- My best mistake
- Famous failures

Think Positive
- A positive mindset
- Half-full or half-empty
- All or nothing
- Celebrate
- Thanks for everything
- Smile!
- Truly positive
- Let it go
- Feelings detective
- Seeing the future
- Positive people
- Doing good
- Be kind to yourself

Don't Panic
- A calm mindset
- Future friend
- Nervous or excited?
- Trust yourself
- Not a competition
- Panic button
- Reach out
- Everything changes
- Do your research
- What can I do?
- What could go wrong?
- If it does go 'wrong'
- Tomorrow is another day

Build Resilience
- A resilient mindset
- The power of 'yet'
- Effort thermometer
- Digging deeper
- Halfway there
- Try to fail
- Positive practice
- Stronger together
- Change for good
- Seeing the future
- Ups and downs
- Rest and recover
- Get creative

Work Smarter
- Mindsets at work
- Fighting fit
- Get chunking!
- Give it your all
- Activate your brain
- Just right
- Give your brain a chance
- Keep repeating
- Nobody's perfect
- How do they do it?
- Know yourself
- Work smart, play smart
- Be the teacher!

Face Your Fears
- Fear and mindsets
- What are you afraid of?
- Meet your fears
- You're not alone
- Being brave
- Little steps
- Big leaps
- Now isn't then
- Story time's over!
- Give it a minute
- See the other side
- Energy swap
- A year from today

Ask For Help
- Help and mindsets
- Everyone needs help
- Be brave
- Speaking up
- No stupid questions
- Who can help?
- Helping others
- Team power
- Taking feedback
- Sharing opinions
- Working through challenges
- Reaching out
- Helping yourself

FRANKLIN WATTS